Midsummer Queen

LIANA BROOKS

OTHER WORKS

HEROES AND VILLAINS

Even Villains Fall In Love
Even Villains Go To The Movies
Even Villains Have Interns
Even Villains Play The Hero (books 1 – 3 omnibus)
The Polar Terror

TIME AND SHADOWS MYSTERIES

The Day Before
Convergence Point
Decoherence

FLEET OF MALIK

Bodies In Motion
Change of Momentum
For Every Action (forthcoming)

Find other works by the author at
www.lianabrooks.com

Midsummer Queen

INKLET #4

LIANA BROOKS

Inkprint PRESS

www.inkprintpress.com

Print ISBN: 978-1-925825-04-6
eBook ISBN: 9781386710714

www.inkprintpress.com

National Library of Australia Cataloguing-in-Publication Data
Liana Brooks 1982 –
Midsummer Queen
34 p.
ISBN: 978-1-925825-04-6
Inkprint Press, Canberra, Australia
1. Fiction—Fantasy—Dark Fantasy 2. Fiction—
Short Stories

First Print Edition: February 2019
Cover design © Inkprint Press
Interior art © Amy Laurens

MIDSUMMER QUEEN

I NEVER UNDERSTOOD THE ONES WHO said they feared the night. Light was the harbinger of evil in my world. The night gave me strength to live. Under the moonlight, I had no bruises.

Midsummer was the worst. Long days shortened the hours of my freedom. I despised the spring blossoms, hated that the night was quickening away.

Sometimes I prayed for an early winter. Deep frost, snow, hunger, starvation... none of those mattered if I could wrap myself in a blanket of darkness.

It is noon by the sundial and the garden is in full bloom. Summer solstice lanterns are hanging through-out the town and from the caverns of the kitchen I can hear the bickering of two old woman. Years of jealousy spill between them, a vile acid that's etched itself into the stone.

From the balcony above, I hear the snide mocking of a second pair who feed on that acid hatred and give it life in their bosoms. Daylight makes a solemn mockery of all I love.

Quietly, I pull my sleeve down to hide the handprints that blacken my flesh. Others think I wear the sleeves out of vanity, that I hide my moon-pale skin from the sun because I reject summer's golden glow.

It is not true. Had I no horror to hide, I too would embrace the sun. But how can I when it is nothing more to me than the witch's pyre?

"Iulia!" A maid calls my name and I am stolen from the gardens to the goblin's den.

Beautiful as the first spring morning is the woman I have called Mother all my life. She is radiant and fair to behold. Praised by men, idolized by artists, all who see her bow in awe.

They should tremble in fear, for that fair face hides a cruelty like no other. Not even a cat tormenting a mouse matches her for cold-hearted pain.

I bow before her, fearing the lash of both her whip and her tongue.

"You are an ugly child." She has said so all my life.

"Forgive me. I know no other way to be."

Her gold slippers glitter in the sunlight as she stalks around me, a lioness looking for a weakness. "When I was your age there were men that avowed they would die if they could not dance with me. Kings went to war to win my hand. Maidens took their own lives because they saw me and knew they could never compare."

"M'lady is the greatest wonder of the modern world," I said. "Not even the sun is more radiant than she." This is the prayer I learned in childhood. My scripture is a paean of praise to the woman I hate most.

"Who would see my beauty slip away?"

"No one, my queen. The world would die for want of you."

"True." A leather crop caresses my cheek. It is her form of endearment. "Once I hoped you would reign beside me, the Little Queen. The moon to my sun. But it cannot be."

The cold leather digs into my cheek and I feel hot blood well up where the rough edge cuts me. "M'lady has other daughters, both radiant and fair."

All are dead.

The gravestones border the garden like a white marble fence. No beauty that competes with her is allowed to live. Yet she births daughters like a queen bee, always searching for her destruction. It makes her feel alive.

"Tonight we will have visitors to help us celebrate the solstice. Won't that be nice?"

Victims for the altar. Suitors from abroad. "They are lucky indeed that the most beautiful of all women allows them to walk in her presence." No matter what my heart feels, I must keep to the well-worn script.

The leather crop strikes across my back, a brief riff of pain between my shoulder blades. "Go. Make yourself presentable. Our guests will be on the altar before the sun sets."

So it is every year. Her sacrifice to the elder gods.

Her assurance of power and beauty.

I flee the room and catch a glimpse of myself in the mirror. Pale skin, white as a winter moon, with hot red blood crusting on my cheek. My pale green dress is marked by the same blood on my back. My hair, crimson as my blood, is matted and filthy.

Still, I lift my chin as I walk. The moon is rising, a pale assassin in the sky, and I can feel the strength it gives me.

No one marks my appearance. The servants never rush to help me. The queen only meets out punishment deserved. Why else would she beat her only living child?

In the cool darkness of my room near the dungeons, I bathe. The water sluices over me, washing away pain and fear.

Resolution strengthens my sinews. Tonight, the moon rises early.

Tonight, I too will ascend, either to flee this golden kingdom or to stand upon the altar as a sacrifice myself; I do not care. All I wish to do is escape the woman who gave me life. The woman who makes my every nightmare truth.

The bells ring in the square. The visitors are here. For them, I shed no tears. Greed led them here, or lust perhaps. The wealthy widow queen whose beauty is beyond compare. They come to claim her, to take what is not theirs. In return, she takes their lives to lengthen her own.

"Iulia." Her voice crawls through the darkness like a spider.

"Mother." I step out in my pale gray dress. My crimson hair is bound up under a dark gold veil. Tonight I am no more than a statue in my mother's menagerie.

Her cold fingers grasp my chin through the veil. "Do you not love me, child? Have I not given you everything, laid aside my own desires to see you well? When you were ill, was it not I who sacrificed everything to win the favor of the elder gods and see you healed? Your father would have let you die, but what did I do?"

"You saved me."

"Yes, I saved you. I gave up everything I held precious so I could see you live."

How generous were the elder gods to give her endless life when all she asked for was a child's health...

But this I do not say. I did once, and I learned how long it takes for bones to mend. "You are more generous than I can say," I whisper.

"Come, child. Walk with me. Our visitors must see how much I love my child."

The stone walls feel like a tomb, although I know my life will end in fire.

One day my mother will tire of me. One day she will cease to toy with me and will slit my throat. Drink my blood.

One day, she will offer me to the elder gods to capture another season in the sun.

Our footfalls lead to the garden, then down to the gate, and finally to the long white path to the square. The setting sun warms our backs.

To the people waiting, we are but two figures—one glowing and golden, one dark and severe—walking out of the light.

They wait, hearts racing in their chests. The queen's magic stretches out, ensnaring them, entangling them in their own wanton wishes.

I look up at the high and pale moon. The sun is falling. The moon reigns.

Almost unbidden, the silver knife appears in my hand, hidden by the fall of my sleeve.

Beside me, my mother pauses. Sunlight dances along the knife edge and the whole world holds still. Which heart calls to this blade? Whose blood will drip from its curving silver tip?

"Iulia?" My mother looks so confused. "Whatever have I done to you, child, to make you hate me so?"

The blade leaps for her throat and I whisper, "Everything." I am free.

THE MAKING OF
MIDSUMMER QUEEN

It was a windy, angry night.

I don't remember now what triggered the anger, I just remember the feeling of being trapped and desperately, violently wanting to escape.

There was nothing to escape from though, except for the depression leeching my mind of joy. So I gave the depression a face, and a name, and then I stabbed it in the back and went to bed laughing.

DOWNLOAD YOUR FREE EBOOK

When you buy a print book from Inkprint Press, we like to say THANK YOU by offering you the ebook for free!

Please head to www.inkprintpress.com/inklets/4/ and the use the coupon INKLET4 to get your copy of this Inklet in epub AND mobi today!
(Coupon will only work once.)

Read more by Liana Brooks!

FLEET OF MALIK
BODIES IN MOTION
CHAPTER ONE

THE PROBLEM WITH VACATIONS, Selena reflected as she adjusted her sweater outside Cargo Blue, was that reality was always waiting at the end. A quick search of the local security cameras found one that showed the peeling sunburn on her right shoulder blade.

Such was the curse of pale-skinned, ship-born Fleet personnel. Anytime she left the foggy belts covering the city of Tarrin, she barbecued like a shrimp, no matter how much sunscreen she applied. Otherwise, she'd flee even further from the Fleet Enclave and make her home on the equatorial beaches of the planet they were trapped on.

She panned the camera and checked her left shoulder. Black ink made a star-scape that disguised three silver scars as shooting stars. The painting covered her shoulder blade and part of her upper arm. As the artist had promised, the skin-paint had kept her from burning as much, though it still had the over-stretched feel of a burn. With a few adjustments, her uniform covered most of the temporary art; it would keep her from having to explain to her colleagues.

Her forearm warmed, a warning that someone was about to contact her through the tech implant tucked between her radius and ulna.

She hesitated too long and the call came through, a persistent ping against her skull as the phantom image of her best friend floated on the edge of her vision.

Selena turned off the visual receiver and answered. "Genevieve," she said with a smile as the image of her vivacious, red-headed friend appeared floating against the backdrop of landing gear that supported the grounded fleet.

A grounder would have thought she was talking to herself, but grounders wouldn't set foot near the neo-city-state of

Enclave. The rocky beach served as a city and tomb for the survivors of the last war.

"Selena!" Gen gushed. "Starcom to Selena. Where are you? I'm covering for now."

"Delayed, but almost there." Selena hoped Gen wouldn't hear the lie. She'd been standing in the shadows of the Enclave pub for nearly a quarter hour.

"The *Lorenza* could get here faster," Gen said, referencing a long-dead ship whose crew were found skeletonized at their stations. Gen blew hair off her face. "Stars above, you're an hour late. The whole fleet is flying faster than you."

Selena turned on her visual long enough to roll her eyes at her friend. "Ha, ha, funny. That joke needs to be forcibly retired." Sooner rather than later. The fleet couldn't fly without fuel, and the Malik system they were stranded in held precious few deposits of the orun crystals needed to power the ships.

"If you don't come," Gen said threateningly, "I will teleport to your apartment and drag you out in your pajamas."

"I'm not at home," Selena admitted. And she wouldn't have let her best friend come to her new house if she was.

Gen was smart enough to realize that the small palace Selena had bought in downtown Tarrin wasn't paid for by her official OIA salary. The paygrades for the Office of Imperial Affairs had last been updated when the Malik system was still in contact with the empire, making them 900 years out of date.

Technically, taking a second job wasn't treason, but there were enough people in the fleet who'd see it as a betrayal that keeping it secret felt right. Especially since Gen's captain was one who would scream the loudest.

Gen clapped. "Selena! Stop stalling yer engines and get in here. This isn't some Fleet Tribunal, just our friends. You, me, Carver. I left a message for Marshall. You know. People we like."

The light of understanding dawned. "Carver? This is so you can snuggle up to Perrin Carver without your parents watching?"

"Yes," Gen admitted, not looking the least bit contrite.

"You're only dragging me along so I can cover for you while you make out in a corner, aren't you?" She masked the relief with mock anger. At least Gen wasn't trying to set Selena up with one of her cousins. Or, ancestors forbid, Gen's handsy older brother.

Again.

Gen opened her eyes wide with an innocent smile. "Maybe."

"Gen!" Selena rolled her eyes. "Doesn't he have his own place?"

"Just the bachelor's dorm. The Carvers didn't have any ships except the shuttle his parents crashed in. Making out next door to Mom and Dad? No. And the BOQ? It's so tacky. You can hear everything through those walls."

Selena hid a smile. "I'll be there soon enough."

If Gen ever caught wind of how panicky the thought of a relationship made her, Gen would make it her life's goal to see Selena paired off. And there wasn't a man alive who she could imagine getting close to now.

Her implant helpfully pulled up an image of a tall, broad-shouldered, lean-muscled fighter with skin black as the night between stars and emerald-green eyes.

She pushed the memory away.

Lieutenant Commander Titan Sciarra was striking, intelligent, and had a body she'd cross battle lines for, but he was also out of reach. There was no point in chasing a man who wouldn't give her the time of day.

Another crew shuffled past her into the bar, black patches with silver fists on their shoulders.

It was getting harder to pretend she belonged in Enclave, with the fleet. Once upon a time, she'd known every crew's patch without thinking. She could name captains, their ships and their seconds by rote.

Now she would need to tap into the fleet's information nexus if she wanted to know who they were.

She stopped at the edge of the door to tug her lightest shields into place. A few minor adjustments would keep bugs away, keep beer off her clothes, and prevent anyone from hacking into her implant. They could still send messages, because disallowing that would have raised eyebrows. And they could still hit her. But she could always hit back.

Selena rolled her shoulders and strutted into Cargo Blue. It was a battlefield, but she was the last captain of the Caryll family, and she wasn't going down without a fight.

Whatever crew owned Cargo Blue probably hadn't had much of a decorating budget, but at least they'd stuck with a theme: oversized cargo boxes were piled up to make walls, seating, and tables. Olive-green safety webbing draped from the ceiling between blue lights. Fog used for fire drills on the ships pumped across the floor to hide the concrete beneath.

There was no bouncer at the door, but people were still hanging around the entrance.

As a rule, the fleet was cautious, and the young faces she saw belonged to fleet members who had never ventured outside their own crew more than a few times, even though the fleet had been grounded for nearly three years.

Tables to the left, bar ahead, dance floor to the right... and that meant the back half of the cargo hanger had been partitioned and karaoke would be in the back right corner. After a few minutes of weaving through the human crush, she found Gen, already sitting in Perrin Carver's lap and giggling.

"Selena!" Gen jumped up and hugged her. "I was beginning to worry!"

"How many people are in here?" Selena shouted over the music.

"Everyone under forty?" Gen laughed. With a small hand wave Gen put up a minor sound shield, muting the music. "People are going to stir crazy. Combine that with the anniversary—"

The anniversary.

Today.

The day the war had begun, the day the

united fleet had died.

They'd been dying for four hundred years, well aware that the reserve of orun crystals was depleted and there was no way to move forward with the ships they had.

Old Captain Baular had seen the deposit of orun on the fifth planet as their saving grace. He'd get it even if it meant killing the grounders.

And, coward that he was, he'd ordered his grandson to lead the first attack instead of leading it himself.

That opening skirmish began and ended in the dark, with Titan Sciarra in the infirmary, and five Academy fighters mis-sing or damaged. But by lunch of the next day, every officer belonging to crews allied with the Baulars withdrew.

Seven months later, heated words turned to live rounds.

"Selena?" Gen asked quietly, placing a hand on her arm. "You didn't know the date, did you?"

"I was trying not to think about." If she had, she'd have cut her vacation to the islands early. Maybe even made her pilgrimage to the small cay where she'd ditched her stolen fighter after driving off the attack.

She rolled her shoulder, stretching the deep scars. "It snuck up on me."

"First round, we drink to the Lost Fleet, and all who've gone on to crew it. I'm buying," Gen said with a touch of forced joviality. "Carver's been making friends. Tell her, babe." She pushed Carver's shoulder.

Perrin Carver was tall, broad-shouldered man with shy, hazel eyes that hid a wicked sense of humor.

Selena's heart fluttered just a little at the memory of a time when she'd fancied herself in love with him. He'd been the ideal starsider: intelligent, good-looking, and charismatic. They'd been friends of a sort, but even that relationship had soured when she'd realized he'd been getting close to her so he could learn more about Genevieve Silar.

Carver nodded and held out his hand. "Hi, Selena. How are you?"

She tapped the back of his hand with hers, letting him test her shields. "Good. How's the Starguard?"

"Booming." The commander of the Starguard smiled, white teeth flashing, but there was a tightness around his eyes. "Everyone hears about guardians being allowed outside the Enclave, or working with the Jhandarmi, and I'm drowning in recruiting requests. Captains of larger crews invite me to Captain's Mess so they can introduce me to their best and brightest. Half the time I can't tell if they want me to marry into the crew or take the fleetlings into the guard." His shield was still attached to hers, scanning her as he talked.

All he would get from her was polite interest. Her heartrate didn't spike or dip at the mention of the Jhandarmi. Her smile never flickered.

"Maybe you should lock down Gen," Selena said. "If you had a spouse, no one would try to get you to marry into the crew."

Carver and Gen shared a look, and Gen

sent a ping of information that Selena's implant translated as an ongoing debate over crew name and a place to live.

Carver sent something similar; a picture of his bachelor's quarters and his one ship.

There was no room for them to marry and have a family.

"Enclave is a temporary solution," Selena said out loud. She'd lost the taste for communicating by implant years ago. "If we—"

A heavy hand wrapped around her waist as someone wearing too much cologne stepped far too close to her. "Hello, Selena."

Hollis Silar, one of Gen's many siblings, kissed her temple.

Simultaneously, Selena sighed, sent a shock through her shield to Hollis's hand, and elbowed him in the gut. "Hi, Hollis. I see you're still bathing in cologne rather than water."

He stepped away from her, an easy smile still in place.

It wasn't that Hollis was bad looking;

plenty of women found him handsome.

It was that he was equally affectionate with every woman he saw and he couldn't keep a secret to save his life. Or anyone else's.

He'd chase anyone with a pretty smile and fell in and out of love a couple of times a day.

"Nice to see you too, Selena. Now, everyone, you're all going to look at me, smile, and laugh like I'm my normal, dashing self," he said, his smile never changing. "You haven't been paying attention, but I'm not a member of the Starguard for nothing. We're being watched. Now take your nice drinks from the waitress and keep your eyes on me."

Hollis nodded to the waitress and handed out four cups with bright purple liquid. "Bruised Stars all around. Guaranteed to make you giggle, or so the guy at the bar told me. Although he's a Seutaai, so take it with a shield in place." He handed Selena her drink with a smile, but turned immediately to glance over his shoulder.

"Big brother, who are we looking for?" Gen asked with a slow drawl. "Is it a friend who you might have forgotten to call back after a night out?"

Hollis shook his head. "No, I thought I saw some of the Lee crew. Make that, I'm certain of it."

Selena grimaced. "As long as Rowena isn't here."

"Did you call me?"

Startled, Selena looked up to the face of her least favorite woman: Rowena Lee.

"Hello," Selena said politely. "I see you're still alive. That's..."

Unfortunate.

She nodded and took a slug of her Bruised Star.

Rowena held up a tray of electric blue shots. "My crew thinks I can't out-drink anyone in this bar. I probably can't go toe-to-toe with alcoholics like the Silars here. But No-Shot Selena?" Rowena set the drinks on the table. "I can out-shoot you in the stars or on the ground."

Gen sucked in air between her teeth and sent Selena several urgent pings telling her to ignore the Lees.

Selena muted Gen. "I took plenty of shots in the war. As I recall, I disabled three of your big birds. *Bassi, Aryton, Theoano…* Bang, bang, bang." Selena mimed firing with her finger. "Three shots. Three silent ships."

"Not kills," Rowena said. "A whole war and you never blooded yourself."

That was it, the memory she didn't want to face; the time she'd almost taken Death's claim and risked killing someone outside of war.

"That's uncalled for," Hollis said, trying to step between them. "Selena, why don't we—"

Selena pushed Hollis aside and grabbed the first shot.

She tossed back the potent drink and shattered the glass on the table. "Go suck vacuum, Rowena. You're a pissant yeoman with no hope of command."

"I went to the Academy, same as you, Selena. I fought for the fleet." Rowena slammed a shot back. "You fought for the mud-lickers."

Selena took another shot as the first started to fuzz her judgement. "I prevented the Baulars from committing mass genocide and destroying the civilians along with the fleet."

Rowena took her second shot. A crowd was gathering and that seemed to feed her cruelty. "The Lees survived the war. We're still here. How many Caryll captains are there? Oh, right, one. Can you count that high, No-Shot? You have any idea how easy it would be for me to end you right now?"

Selena took the last two glasses and slammed them both back.

Gen pinged her, giving locations, counts, and identities of the Lee allies in the crowd.

Hollis stepped to her flank, ready to defend her.

She stood, anger burning through her veins. "Sure, your crew outnumbers mine. I guess on paper, it's not really a fair fight, is it, Rowena? But you were trained as a flight leader, and what do Carylls do? Hand-to-hand combat. Maybe I should thin your ranks, starting with one mouthy yeoman."

Keep reading! Head to: http://www.inkprintpress.com/liana-brooks/newtons-laws/bodies-in-motion/

ABOUT THE AUTHOR

LIANA BROOKS is not an immortal who has forgotten more than a human mind can hope to learn in one lifetime, she just sounds like one.

If you ignore her archaic vocabulary and fondness for century-long naps, she's an ordinary author living in the Pacific Northwest with her family and her giant dog, who is absolutely not named Cerberus.

She has written the popular *Time and Shadows Mysteries* series about clones and the dangers of time travel; the *Fleet of Malik* series of connected sci-fi romances about re-building after a decades long war; and the cult-following *Heroes and Villains* series of superhero romances.

You can find out more about Liana at her website, www.lianabrooks.com.

INKLETS

Collect them all! Released on the 1st and 15th of each month.

SEVENTY
LIANA BROOKS
A Final Request for Mercy
AMY LAURENS
the kitten psychologist
vs.
the kitten's owners
THEA VAN DIEPEN
Answer the Question
AMY LAURENS
Happily, Red
AMY LAURENS
the kitten psychologist
tries to be patient
through email
THEA VAN DIEPEN
DRAGON Tuesday
AMY LAURENS
RED PLANET REFUGEES
LIANA BROOKS
the kitten psychologist &
What The Kitten Did
THEA VAN DIEPEN

Cherry Blossom
AMY LAURENS
Alone
AMY LAURENS
the kitten psychologist & The Kitten Come To A Conclusion
THEA VAN DIEPEN
LEVEL NINE
LIANA BROOKS
To Dust
AMY LAURENS
Interchange
AMY LAURENS
Emalia's Lanterns
LIANA BROOKS
Dear Santa
AMY LAURENS
The Quilt-Maker's Scrap
AMY LAURENS